Brady Brady and the Twirlin' Torpedo

Written by Mary Shaw

Illustrated by Chuck Temple

Visit **www.bradybrady.com** for more Brady Brady information

Published in Canada in 2004 by

Brady Brady Inc.
P.O. Box 367
Waterloo, Ontario
Canada
N2J 4A4

Canadian Cataloguing in Publication Data

ISBN 0-9735557-2-6

Brady and the other Icehogs support Tes when she is ridiculed for being the only girl player on the team.

Printed and bound in Canada

Keep adding to your Brady Brady book collection! Other titles include **Brady Brady and the:**

- **Great Rink**
- **Runaway Goalie**
- **Missed Hatrick**
- **Singing Tree**
- **Super Skater**
- **Big Mistake**
- **Great Exchange**
- **Most Important Game**
- **MVP**
- **Puck on the Pond**
- **Cranky Kicker**
- **B Team**
- **Ballpark Bark**
- **Cleanup Hitters**

For my daughter,
Taylore Elizabeth Shaw
Mary Shaw

To my sisters,
Cathy and Gayle
Chuck Temple

Brady ***loved*** hockey. So did his friend Tes. When they weren't with the other Icehogs, they were usually on Brady's backyard rink, practicing slapshots or stuffing pucks past Hatrick.

Brady thought it was great that a girl ***loved*** hockey as much as he did.

At first, some of the Icehogs wondered about having a girl on the team. That was before the Coach got Tes to show them her “Twirlin’ Torpedo.”

She…

leapt into the air,
twirled in a full circle, landed,
and fired the puck with all her might!

Chester never even saw it coming. Tes had always hated her figure skating lessons, but those spins had finally come in handy. She was welcomed to the team, and now she was an Icehog like the rest of them.

Today, the Icehogs were playing an ***annoying*** team called the Hounds.
Brady had been up since the crack of dawn.

He liked to be first at the rink so he could high-five
his teammates as they arrived.
As usual, Tes was the next one through the door.

When everyone was there and ready to play, the Icehogs huddled in the center of the dressing room for their team cheer.

"We've got the power,
We've got the might,
We've got the spirit . . .
Those Hounds won't bite!"

Both teams took their positions on the ice.
The referee dropped the puck and play began.
It was then that Brady and the others heard the teasing.

"What's a ***girl*** doing out here? Go home to your mommy," sneered one of the Hounds.

“Did you tie your skates in a pretty bow?” hollered another. “Why don’t you go home and play with your dolls?”

Brady looked at Tes. She just continued to play. If she heard the heckling, she was doing a great job of ignoring it.

“Don’t listen,” Brady said
when he sat on the bench beside Tes.
“You’re as good a player as anyone here.”

“Don’t worry, Brady Brady. I’m ***not*** going to let them get to me!”
Tes replied.

But when she went out for her next shift, the teasing continued.
And it got louder.

"Go home and bake some cookies!" yelled a Hound.

"Make sure you don't break a nail!" barked his friend.

The taunts continued through the entire first period and into the second. Brady watched Tes. She was biting her bottom lip.

As hard as she tried,
Tes could not ignore the Hounds.
She couldn't concentrate. She missed passes.
She skated in the wrong direction.
She even tripped over the blueline!

When Tes tried her "Twirlin' Torpedo,"
she fanned on the puck and fell down in a heap.
The Hounds laughed even harder.

The buzzer sounded to end the second period,
and Tes was first off the ice.

In the dressing room, nobody knew what to say.
Tes looked sadly down at her skates.
"I guess I let you guys down," she whispered.

"No way! Nobody could play with all
that teasing going on!" Chester said.

"Right!" the other Icehogs chimed in.
"We'd be exactly the same, if it was us."

"Wait!" cried Brady. "That gives me a ***great*** idea!"

"All right, Brady Brady!"
The team huddled together to hear Brady's plan.

When the Icehogs skated out for the final period,
the Hounds just stood there with their mouths hanging open.
Some even rubbed their eyes to make sure they
weren't seeing things.

The Icehogs had a new look!
They had flipped their jerseys inside out,
tucked their hair up, and disguised their faces.

It was impossible to tell who was who!

"Let's play hockey!" Brady shouted, and the Icehogs flew into action.
They had never played so well – or laughed so much during a game!

The Hounds stopped teasing Tes because they couldn't tell which player she was!

Until . . .

. . . she lined up the puck
at the blueline,

leapt into the air,
twirled in a full circle,
landed,
and fired the puck with all her might!

Her “Twirlin’ Torpedo” sailed right into the top corner of the Hounds’ net, seconds before the buzzer sounded to end the game.

Tes had scored the winning goal!

The teams lined up to shake hands.
This time, the Hounds were first to skate off the ice with ***their*** heads hanging.

“Maybe they’ve gone looking for a girl to help them out,” chuckled Brady, as he high-fived Tes.

Just then, the Hounds' goalie came back onto the ice. He skated over to Tes. "Great game," he said.

"You mean, for a ***girl?***" asked Tes.

"No. I mean ***you*** played a great game."

And a crowd of funny faces nodded in agreement.